Nothing Else But Yams For Supper!

Nothing Else But Yams For Supper was published in October 1988 by Black Moss Press, 1939 Alsace Ave., Windsor, Ontario, Canada N8W1M5. Black Moss books are distributed in Canada and the U.S. by Firefly Books, Scarborough, Ontario. All orders should be directed there.

Black Moss books are published with the assistance of the Canada Council and the Ontario Arts Council.
This book was designed by Jirina Marton.

Printed in Canada by The National Press, Toronto, Ontario.

ISBN 0-88753-182-2

NOTHING ELSE BUT YAMS FOR SUPPER!

Story by Joan Buchanan
Illustrations by Jirina Marton

Black Moss Press

Alice liked yams for supper. Nothing else would do but yams for supper because nothing else was as soft and mucky and yummy as yams.

Her mother pleaded, "Alice, please eat your meat!"

But Alice said, "No, all I want is yams for supper. Nothing else is as soft and mucky and yummy as yams!" So all Alice ate was yams for supper.

Her brother laughed and said, "Have some of my peanut butter, bacon and banana sandwich. It's really gooey."

But Alice said, "No! All I want is yams. Nothing else is as soft and mucky and yummy."

Alice's father said, "Look here, I'll give you a chocolate bar."

But Alice said, "No!"

Alice and her family went on a big trip. First they went to Finland. At the restaurant, the waiter shrugged and said, "Sorry, no yams!"

Alice was angry! "What? No yams? But that's all I eat! All I want is yams for supper. Nothing else is as soft and mucky and yummy as yams!"

Alice went out. She searched the streets and stores for yams. She looked and looked. She couldn't find any yams at all.

Alice was getting tired and hungry. Then she saw a specialty shop. "Maybe there will be yams in here," she said.

The storekeeper said, "Sorry, no yams. How about some chestnuts or Finnish mints or tender reindeer steak?"

Alice said, "All I want is yams! Nothing else is as soft and mucky and yummy."

Now Alice was very tired and hungry. She ran back to the restaurant and she told the waiter, "Have you got anything as soft and yummy as yams for supper?"

The waiter said, "Yes, we've got reindeer meatballs in thick gravy. There's creamed potatoes and chestnut mousse for dessert."

Alice was so very, very hungry that she tried the chestnut mousse. She was glad she did. It was soft and mucky and yummy. Her family clapped and cheered.

Then she travelled to China.

At the restaurant, Alice ordered yams. The waiter sighed and said, "Sorry, no yams."

Alice was angry! "What? No yams?! But that's all I eat! All I want is yams for supper. Nothing else is as soft and mucky and yummy as yams! Oh, except for chestnut mousse. Do you have that?"

"No," said the waiter.

Alice went out. She searched the streets and stores for yams. She looked and looked. She couldn't find any yams at all.

Alice was getting tired and hungry. Then she saw a big market. "Maybe there will be some yams in there," she said.

The grocer said, "Sorry, no yams, not at this time of the year. How about some bean sprouts, or fresh fish, or bamboo shoots?"

Alice said, "All I want is yams! Nothing else is as soft and mucky and yummy."

Now Alice was very tired and hungry. She ran back to the restaurant and she said to the waiter, "Have you got anything as soft and mucky and yummy as yams for supper?"

The waiter said, "Yes, we've got bean curd in black bean sauce, soft steamed buns and lemon chicken."

Alice was so very, very hungry that she tried the bean curd in black bean sauce. She was glad she did. It was soft and mucky and yummy. Her family clapped and cheered. They smiled at each other.

Then they went to Mexico.

At the restaurant, Alice ordered yams. The waiter shook his head. "Sorry, no yams."

Alice was angry! "What! No yams?! But that's all I eat. All I want is yams for supper. Nothing else is as soft and mucky and yummy as yams! Oh, except for chestnut mousse and bean curd and black bean sauce. Do you have those?"

"No," said the waiter.

Alice went out. She searched the streets and stores for yams. She looked and looked. She couldn't find any yams at all.

Alice was getting tired and hungry. Then she saw a big supermarket. "Maybe, there will be some yams in there," she said.

The manager said, "Sorry, we're all sold out today. How about some chilis, or tortillas, or avocadoes?"

Alice said, "All I want is yams. Nothing else is as soft and mucky and yummy."

Now Alice was very tired and hungry. She ran back to the restaurant and she said to the waiter, "Have you got anything as soft and mucky and yummy as yams for supper?"

The waiter said, "Yes, we've bean burritos, beef tacos and guacamole."

Alice was so very, very hungry that she tried guacamole. She was glad she did. It was soft and mucky and yummy.

"Wow!" Alice said, "Now I like chestnut mousse, bean curd in black bean sauce and guacamole. Isn't it wonderful there is so much to eat in this world that's as soft and mucky and yummy as yams?"